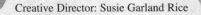

Creative Director: Susie Garland Rice

Dalmatian Press owns all art and editorial material.
ISBN: 1-57759-256-5
© 1999 Dalmatian Press. All rights reserved.
Printed and bound in the U.S.A. The DALMATIAN
PRESS name, logo and spotted spine are trademarks of
Dalmatian Press, Franklin, Tennessee 37067.

Written permission must be secured from the publisher to
use or reproduce any part of this book.

10654a/Jack and the Beanstalk

Jack and the Beanstalk

Illustrated by David Wariner

Adapted by Ashley Crownover

Dalmatian Press

Once upon a time there was a poor widow and her only son, Jack. Life had been hard ever since an evil giant killed Jack's father and stole the family's treasures. All Jack and his mother had left was their milking cow. One day Jack's mother said sadly, "Jack, you must take the cow to market and sell her. We have nothing left to eat."

Jack loved his cow and didn't want to sell her, but he knew there was no other choice. So he set out early the next day for market.

On the way, Jack met a strange old man who offered him five beautiful rainbow-colored beans in exchange for the cow. "They're magic!" the man said. Jack eagerly agreed to the trade.

Jack ran home to show his mother the wonderful beans. But when he told her what had happened, she was very angry. "Trading a cow for five worthless beans!" she said. "Now we'll starve!" She threw the beans out the window, and they both went to bed hungry.

When Jack woke the next morning, he found that an enormous beanstalk had sprung up outside the window. He quickly began to climb it, going higher and higher, until at last he reached the top.

There Jack saw an enormous castle. A woman answered the castle door, and Jack said, "I am very hungry. Can you give me something to eat?" "No!" said the woman. "Go away! My husband, the Giant, will eat you!" But Jack begged, and finally the Giant's wife let him in. Just then they heard a loud thump, thump, thump. "He's coming!" the woman cried. "Hide in the oven!" Jack jumped into the oven.

The Giant came in shouting, "Fee, fie, fo, fum, Look out, Human, here I come! Eyes, ears, hands and feet, I smell something good to eat!"

"Nonsense," said his wife. The Giant sat down and called for his magic hen. "Lay!" he roared, and the hen laid a golden egg. Then the Giant dozed off, and Jack crept out of the oven.

Jack snatched up the hen, and ran away as fast as he could.

Jack and his mother lived happily for a
long time by selling the hen's golden eggs.

Then one day Jack decided to climb the beanstalk again to recover more of the family's treasures.

He disguised himself and returned to the castle. "No," said the Giant's wife when she came to the door. "The last time I fed a boy, he stole my husband's hen."

But Jack begged, and the Giant's wife let him in. Just then they heard a loud thump, thump, thump. "Quick!" said the Giant's wife. "Hide in this kettle!"

The Giant came in shouting, "Fee, fie, fo, fum, Look out, Human, here I come! Eyes, ears, hands and feet, I smell something good to eat!" "You're always saying that," his wife replied. "Come eat your supper."

After supper, the Giant got out his enchanted harp. "Play!" commanded the Giant, and the golden harp began to play all by itself. After a while, the Giant began to snore. Jack jumped out of the kettle and grabbed the harp. The harp cried out, "Master, Master!" The Giant awoke and ran after Jack.

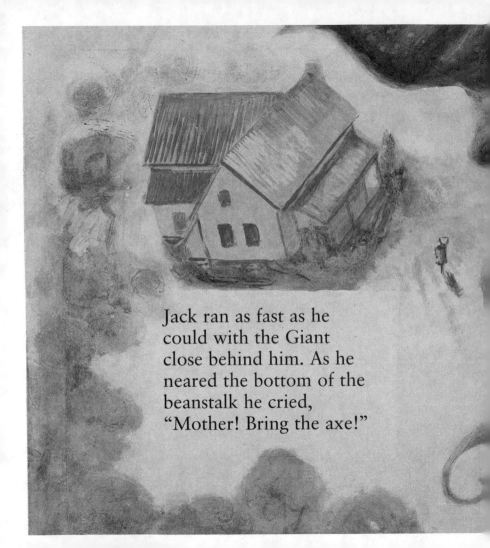

Jack ran as fast as he
could with the Giant
close behind him. As he
neared the bottom of the
beanstalk he cried,
"Mother! Bring the axe!"

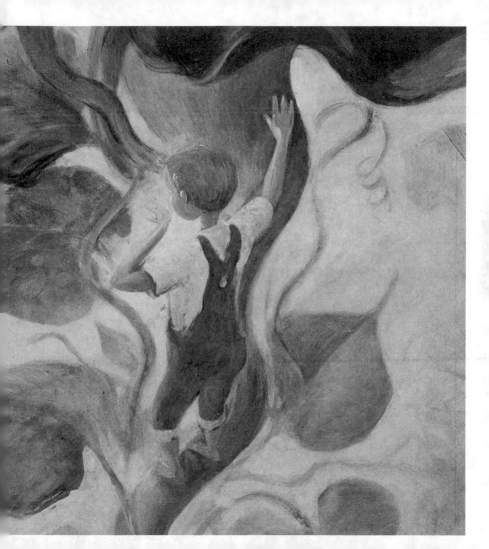

Jack jumped to the ground and took the axe from his mother. He struck the beanstalk as hard as he could.

Down came the beanstalk
and down came the
Giant—dead.

So all ended well for Jack
and his mother, if not for
the Giant. And as for the
wonderful beanstalk, it
never grew again.

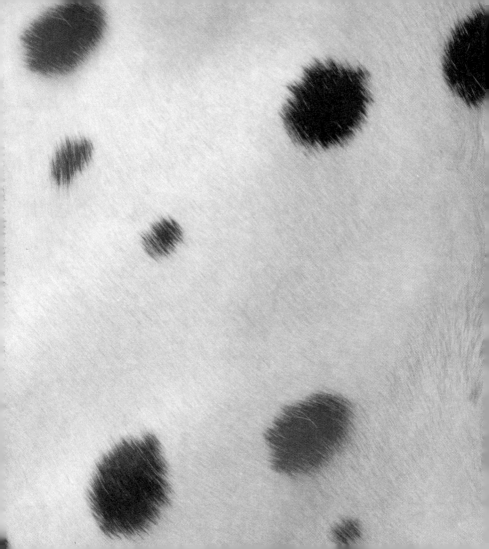